A TIME FOR CHOOSING

MALACHI BOOTH

This is an on-the-run story. The story is about a prince who is constantly opposing a strong marine. It takes place in an archive in a village. The story ends with someone writing a book. The question 'is man alone in the universe' plays a major role.

Contents

Introduction

This is an on-the-run story. The story is about a prince who is constantly opposing a strong marine. It takes place in an archive in a village. The story ends with someone writing a book. The question 'is man alone in the universe' plays a major role.

What's The Story About?

The story is about a cowardly sailor, a wistful video game addict, and a weary salesperson. It takes place in a town in an intergalactic empire. The crux of the story involves an elopement. The issue of gay rights plays a major role in the story.

A Lot OF Short Stories

The story is about elegant chief starship engineers. It starts in an outpost on an arctic planet. The story begins with a political conflict. The religion of the world will turn out not to be what it seems.

Who Was The Knight IN Shining Armor?

The story is about a queen who is engaged to an outlaw. It takes place in a galaxy of magic. The crux of the story involves a reconciliation.

What is a CFO

This is a tale about heroism. The story is about marines. It starts in a prison in a law-abiding dukedom. The crux of the story involves a massacre. Magic is increasing in power, and that plays an important role in the story.

The story is about a construction worker who has a crush on a CFO. It starts in a magical dimension. The crux of the story involves a training. Genetic engineering and its side effects is a major part of this story.

CHAPTER SIX

Like A Tiger, In With A Beast

This is a coming-of-age tale with an emphasis on degeneracy and religion versus science. The story is about a movie reviewer who possesses a strong immunity to magic. It takes place in a hovel in an outpost. The unexpected difficulties technology can bring is a major part of the story.

Never AGAIN

The story is about a healthy anthropologist who is given to moments of deep introspection. It takes place on a swamp planet in a galaxy-spanning commonwealth. The story begins with someone getting a new job and ends with a kidnapping. The gap between the rich and the poor nations plays a major role in this story.

THE END, Could It Be?

Me and Greg did into the classroom. 'Malachi Booth! Greg! Why are you late?' shouted Mr. Matthew 'Because Malachi Booth forgot the Greg's lion got stuck up the giraffe!' 'Well, I don't believe you.' said Matthew, 'You both carrots for the social studies lesson.' said Greg. 'No!' I said, 'It's because have to do 14 2000 detention!'

CHAPTER NINE

CHAPTER TEN

Who Cares?

Polly Meadows looked at the ripped hawk in her hands and felt delighted.

She walked over to the window and reflected on her wild surroundings. She had always loved quiet Los Angeles with its quaint, quarrelsome quarries. It was a place that encouraged her tendency to feel delighted.

Then she saw something in the distance, or rather someone. It was the figure of Steven Donaldson. Steven was an intelligent painter with curvy eyes and greasy lips.

Polly gulped. She glanced at her own reflection. She was a violent, patient, port drinker with curvaceous eyes and short lips. Her friends saw her as a depressed, damaged doctor. Once, she had even made a cup of tea for a gifted baby.

But not even a violent person who had once made a cup of tea for a gifted baby, was prepared for what Steven had in store today.

The clouds danced like singing bears, making Polly shocked.

As Polly stepped outside and Steven came closer, she could see the amused glint in his eye.

"Look Polly," growled Steven, with a virtuous glare that reminded Polly of intelligent toads. "It's not that I don't love you, but I want some more Twitter followers. You owe me 3345 euros."

Polly looked back, even more shocked and still fingering the ripped hawk. "Steven, d'oh," she replied.

They looked at each other with angry feelings, like two long, loopy lizards loving at a very smelly wake, which had classical music playing in the background and two splendid uncles sleeping to the beat.

Suddenly, Steven lunged forward and tried to punch Polly in the face. Quickly, Polly grabbed the ripped hawk and brought it down on Steven's skull.

Steven's curvy eyes trembled and his greasy lips wobbled. He looked worried, his wallet raw like a glorious, grotesque gun.

Then he let out an agonising groan and collapsed onto the ground. Moments later Steven Donaldson was dead.

Polly Meadows went back inside and made herself a nice glass of port.